Her Christmas Surprise

HER CHRISTMAS SURPRISE

Copyright ©2018 by Cheryl Wright

Cover Artist: Black Widow Books

Dedication

To Margaret Tanner, my very dear friend and fellow author, for her enduring encouragement and friendship.

To Alan, my husband of over forty-six years, who has been a relentless supporter of my writing and dreams for many years.

To You, my wonderful readers, who encourage me to continue writing these stories. It is such a joy knowing so many of you enjoy reading my stories as much as I love writing them for you.

Table of Contents

Chapter One

Simone Allen woke to loud tapping on her car window.

"You can't sleep here, lady," the cop yelled through the closed window.

She rubbed the sleep out of her eyes and slowly sat up. Despite the blanket covering her, she was chilled to the bone.

Glancing around, she remembered where she was – about eight hours out of Grand Falls, Montana.

The cop stood his ground, continuing to stare through the window at her, indicating for Simone to wind it down.

She was stiff from too many nights sleeping on the back seat of her old jalopy. She was beyond hungry; she hadn't eaten much for days, and only had a few measly dollars left. Maybe enough to buy breakfast?

She wasn't convinced.

Once that was done, she was dead broke. She had enough gas to get to her destination, but if the job didn't work out, she had no idea how she'd get back home.

But then again, where was home? She'd been roaming for months. With no work, nowhere to live, and very little money, she'd lived the life of a ghost.

She wanted it to end.

Finding that advertisement was like discovering a gold mine. The newspaper was months old when she came across it, but she still gave it a shot.

She'd sent off her application using the local post office as her address. With only limited experience, she applied to be the new cook at the Silver Shoe Ranch in Grand Falls, Montana.

She'd had to stay put until she got the response, but it was worth the wait.

Many days of driving, and no money for hotels if she wanted to eat at all, Simone set out on her great adventure.

And now she was only hours away from learning her fate.

"Sorry, Officer," she said. "I was afraid I'd fall asleep at the wheel, so pulled to the side for a nap."

He nodded but didn't speak.

"I must have been more tired than I realized." She looked at her watch. "I've been asleep for about six hours."

He straightened up. "It's alright, Ma'am. Just be on your way and we'll forget about it." He started to walk away but she called him back.

"Wait!" she shouted to his retreating back. "Where can I get some food? Cheap."

His eyes burned into her, and she swore he could read her mind. "Two blocks down and turn left. The little church there runs meals three times a day. Everyone is welcome."

She felt the heat creep up her face. She'd been through some hard times in her life, but she'd never been quite this desperate.

"Thank you," she said quietly, suddenly aware of just how low she'd fallen.

He tipped his hat and walked away having no idea how much that meal was going to mean to her.

* * *

Simone braced herself against the cold Montana weather.

When she answered that advertisement, she had no idea what she would be getting into.

The little information she knew was gleaned from the letter she received from Vern Hadley, the ranch owner. She knew she was going to be the new ranch cook since their cook of more than twenty years was retiring.

But he didn't say how many she'd be cooking for. She wondered how big his family was – three or four kids and his wife, perhaps? She shivered, not necessarily because of the cold, but wondering if she would stack up to their expectations.

There were going to be very big shoes to fill.

She was worried too, because she'd agreed to a trial period, not a solid job. And she really needed something more secure. She was done with a life of roaming; she was ready to settle down in one place.

She didn't have such a cold location in mind, though.

Upmost in her mind was ensuring she worked hard and secured the position permanently.

Mr Hadley's letter said their current cook, Mrs Simpson, would be there long enough to teach her the ropes, and then she would be gone. Three to four weeks, or perhaps a little longer.

She gulped in the cold air. *How hard could it be? She'd been cooking since she was a teenager. She'd even helped out in the kitchen at the local hotel.*

Simone stood on the porch rubbing her hands together and praying for someone to rescue her from the harsh weather. She lifted her icy cold hand, poised to knock once more.

"Well hello there." She felt the warmth of a roaring fire ooze out the front door, and longed to be next to it. "You must be Simone Allen?"

She nodded, her voice momentarily lost.

The man was around six foot – tall, dark and handsome, and most likely her boss.

Simone shook her head against the thought.

"Come in, come in out of the cold." He motioned her inside. "You must be freezing in that flimsy get-up."

He wasn't wrong, but she had nothing warmer.

"We weren't expecting you until tomorrow.

She continued to rub her hands together. "I made better time than I'd expected." She had no intentions of telling him she'd run out of money. She had to arrive early or not eat for another day. Maybe two.

Unless she found another church or soup kitchen along the way. She wasn't willing to risk it.

She had a death grip on her overnight bag. Practically everything she owned was in it. More importantly, the brooch her mother had given her when she was ten was in that bag.

He nodded and led her into the living room where several people, men, sat around the fire.

"I'm Hank Hadley, by the way," he said, stretching his hand toward her.

She shook his hand, then studied the cozy room with its roaring fire, and comfy looking chairs. It seemed like a real friendly place. Then she noticed the three men staring at her. Looking her up and down, assessing everything about her.

"Your hands are freezing," he said, as if he was telling her something new. "This is my father Vern, and my brothers Nash and Beau."

She approached each one and shook their proffered hands, keeping a tight grip on the bag. "I'm very pleased to meet you all," she said quietly.

"Honestly, Hank," Beau said. "You didn't think to take the lady's luggage?" He was up in a flash and snatched it up from her. She kept a close eye on it. "If you'll follow me, Ma'am,"

"Simone," she said, slightly shaken that her possessions had been whisked away.

He frowned. "If you'll follow me, Ma'am, er, Simone, I'll show you to your room."

"Thank you," she said quietly, a little overwhelmed by it all.

He pushed the door open with his foot and motioned for her to go first. "It's not much," he said. "But it's comfortable, and warm. We look after our staff here at Silver Shoe Ranch."

She looked around, mouth agape. It was better than some of the hotel rooms she'd seen when she worked part-time as a cleaner, way back when she was at high school.

The double bed had an ornate bedhead, and the comforter looked cozy enough she wanted to lay down on it right then and there.

There was a leather chair in the corner, and a small writing desk opposite the bed. A small wardrobe stood next to it.

He placed her bag in a corner, then proceeded to close the curtains. "Make sure you keep these closed overnight, and while you're dressing. *Always* while you're dressing. We have cowboys on this ranch. Lots of them, and they don't often get to see a pretty lady."

He grinned, and it changed his entire face.

"I," Simone wasn't sure what to say at that precise moment. His words had really taken her aback.

"Follow me and I'll show you the bathroom." She worried if she'd remember where everything was, but it seemed easy enough.

They were on their way back to the living room when he declared. "Where are my manners? I didn't even give you time to take the weight off your feet. I do apologize Ma'am. Er, Simone."

Mrs Simpson was handing out hot beverages and offered Simone a warm drink. "Hot chocolate or tea? We don't do coffee at this hour of the night."

Simone laughed. "Who doesn't drink coffee at night?"

All eyes turned to her. "It's a tradition," Beau told her. "It's early to bed, early to rise. You've never worked on a ranch before, have you?"

Was he mocking her? Because it sure felt like he was. Four sets of eyes were suddenly staring at her. She wanted to shrink into the floor boards.

"Don't mind this lot," Mrs Simpson said. "They just ain't used to a refined lady such as yourself." She put her arm around Simone and walked her to the kitchen. "Now's a good as time as any to check out the kitchen."

The entire house was surprisingly warm. After the freezing temperatures she'd endured over the past days, she fully expected it to be cold inside.

Once they reached the kitchen, Mrs Simpson turned to her. "A couple of things you need to know; breakfast is at 5:30."

Simone swallowed. "5:30 AM? In the morning?" She must have heard wrong.

Mrs Simpson laughed. "You've definitely never worked on a ranch before. Have you worked as a cook?" She looked sternly at the younger woman. "I mean, ever?"

Simone took a deep breath, certain she was about to be told to hightail it out of there. "No Ma'am," she said softly. "Apart from a part-time job in the hotel kitchen when I was at high school, this will be my first time."

The older woman laughed. "This could be interesting."

Simone frowned.

"My dear girl, you obviously have no idea what you're getting into. Vern didn't tell you?"

Now Simone was really worried. She'd driven the past four days to get here, sleeping in her car because she didn't have money for a motel room if she wanted to eat. And now it appeared as though she was about to be sacked.

Before she even started.

Hopefully they'd let her stay the night. She'd been looking forward to a warm bed with a comfy mattress.

She was almost too afraid to ask. "Didn't tell me what?"

Something was apparently hilarious because Mrs Simpson looked like she was about to pee her pants she was laughing so much.

"This I gotta see," she said, then proceeded to make a warm drink for Simone. "I'm sorry. It's really not funny." Mrs Simpson pulled herself together and reached for a mug.

"Am I," Simone braced herself. She felt nauseated, and probably would have brought up her supper – if she'd had any. Which she hadn't. "Mrs Simpson," she said abruptly, bile moving up her throat. "Am I going to lose my job?"

The other woman suddenly stopped laughing and put a kindly arm around the young girl. "My dear girl, I am not the one who does the hiring and the firing. That's Mr Hadley."

Simone frowned.

"But I doubt you'll be fired. He's had a hard time getting anyone to come way out here. In fact, you're the only one who answered his advert in months." She squeezed Simone's shoulder. "You're shivering, dear girl. Are you cold?"

"A little, but more scared, I think."

Suddenly she found herself pulled into a warm bear hug. After years of cooking, there were mounds of cuddly all over the older lady. "I didn't mean to scare you." She pushed Simone away and stared into her face.

"Here's the thing – on a ranch we cook breakfast and supper. We bake too. For all the boys." She continued to stare.

"Right." That didn't sound too hard. She'd cooked for her family before. Baked even. "I can do that."

Mrs Simpson frowned at her. "I don't think you understand, girly. Those boys in there? They're not the only ones."

Simone's head was in a whirl? Not the only ones? How many other men were there in this family, and where were they?

"So how many more Hadley's are there?"

"My dear girl," Mrs Simpson said firmly. "I cook for around thirty at each meal."

Simone stood staring at her, eyes opened wide. If she clamped her teeth any tighter, she'd smash them into tiny pieces.

* * *

It was a shock, there was no doubt about, but Simone just had to grin and bear it. There was no other option.

Leaving definitely wasn't an option. With no money, and no other means of support, she was in a very difficult situation.

She sipped her hot chocolate, looking around the room, trying to size up each of the men. It didn't work. Finally, she excused herself, citing the long drive for making her so tired.

Everyone seemed so nice.

"Set your alarm for 4:30," Mrs Simpson had told her. Breakfast is *served* at 5:30 and we have to prepare it much earlier."

It got worse and worse at every turn.

Simone had never gone to bed before eight before. Heck, she'd rarely gone before ten!

She listened to the quiet of night on the ranch. It was so peaceful here. A far cry from the noise of the city.

She lay in bed and listened to wind blow through the trees, to the owls hooting, and to the sound of horses neighing.

It was too quiet. She lay there in the silence, churning things over in her mind. What if she didn't cut it? What if she couldn't cope, or they hated her, or her cooking?

A tear rolled down her cheek, and she was tempted to give in and sob her heart out, but knew the family would hear her, with her room being so close to the living room.

She heard the laughter of four men enjoying themselves, then footsteps and all went quiet. Had they too gone to bed?

The little light that was creeping in under her door was gone. She was suddenly in total blackness.

She crept out of bed and silently locked the door. Simone was suddenly afraid – of her future on Silver Shoe Ranch – but knew, given her circumstances, she would have to suck it up and get on with it.

For now, anyway.

Chapter Two

"We're self sufficient on this ranch," Mrs Simpson told her. "The first thing you need to learn is how to slice bacon off the bone."

She handed over the bacon and the sharpest knife Simone had ever seen.

"I, um," She didn't want to touch the knife, she was sure it would do some serious damage.

Mrs Simpson frowned at her. "Listen, Simone," she said, more than a little annoyed. "You're a nice girl. I don't want to see you lose this job. Watch me."

"You make it look so easy." This time she took the knife and looked to the older woman for reassurance.

"Not too chunky. Keep it reasonably thin." She talked Simone through her first two cuts. "Now try it on your own."

Simone concentrated hard. It wasn't as easy as Mrs Simpson made it seem. "How's that?" She was again looking for reassurance.

"Well done! Now keep going."

Simone yawned. She was so not used to these early mornings. The sun hadn't even risen when her alarm went off, and the house was silent except for the movements of Mrs Simpson making coffee in the kitchen.

"Righto, finish cutting all that lot, then we'll start cooking."

Simone stared at her. "All of it?"

"All of it. We'll have thirty hungry cowboys at the table in as many minutes." She snatched up a basket and headed out the door. "I'm off to collect the eggs. You'll need to do that each morning too, but I'll show you another time." She was a kindly lady, and patted Simone on the back. "You'll get there. I have no doubt about that."

Simone nodded and continued to cut the bacon into slices as Mrs Simpson left.

"Good morning!" It was Beau. How was he so bright and cheery at such an early hour.

"Oh no! I must be running late," she exclaimed at the sight of him.

"Calm down," he said. "I like to rise a little earlier than the others, so I can enjoy my coffee in peace."

He reached over and flipped the jug on, then pulled down a mug and prepared it for his coffee.

The muscles in his back rippled across under his shirt. She couldn't pull her eyes away.

"Would you like one?"

She ripped her eyes back to the job at hand and grimaced. "I'd love one but haven't got time. Thanks though. Maybe later?"

He watched as she struggled with the job at hand. "Here, let me help." He reached over and took the knife.

"Get your damned hands off that knife, young Beau!" Mrs Simpson yelled. "She won't learn with you helping out."

He let go of the knife and threw his hands in the air. "She can be a viper," he whispered, but Simone could see he was having difficulty withholding a smirk.

"I heard that. Make your coffee and get out of my kitchen!"

"But, but, isn't Beau your boss," Simone asked. "How can you kick him out?"

Mrs Simpson glared at her. "Mr Hadley is my boss. Beau is just one of the cowboys. And cowboys don't belong in my kitchen. You best keep that in mind for when it's your kitchen."

Simone gawked. "My kitchen?"

"Yes, your kitchen. You could almost say it's your kitchen now. Almost." Her expression went from being very annoyed back to kindly. "How are you going with that bacon, girly? It's almost time to feed them lot out there."

Simone stretched to look out into the enclosed dining area where the cowboys ate. "Oh heck! There's a ton of them already."

"Don't you mind them. We have a schedule and we stick to it. You still have fifteen minutes. Finish the bacon, then we'll start cooking."

"You're doing good," she added. "I'll get you trained up, don't you worry."

Simone nodded. She didn't have Mrs Simpson's confidence, but hopefully that would change over time.

"I've already filled the urn for that lot's coffee."

Simone looked at her in dismay. How on earth did the older woman manage all this herself.

Mrs Simpson answered the unspoken question. "I fill it at night, then turn it on when I get up. It takes forever to heat up."

Simone wondered if she should be taking notes.

"Righto, done? Good, time to cook." Simone followed Mrs Simpson out to the dining area.

There was a large electric barbeque where breakfast was cooked.

"Listen up you lot," Mrs Simpson yelled, amongst the cat whistles. "This is Simone. She's the new cook." There was a lot of whistling and shouting. "Any of you lot give her grief and I'll kick your ass myself. Got it?" They all hushed.

"Where are you goin' Mrs Simpson?" one cowboy asked.

"Well Joe, I'm retiring. I been here for more than twenty years now, and it's time. I'll train up this little girl, then I'm off."

Until then, Simone hadn't noticed Beau sitting out with the other cowboys. "We'll all miss you Mrs Simpson," he told her. She heard the sincerity in his voice. As tough as she could be, and Simone fully understood why she was like that, she was also a kindly lady.

She instructed Simone how to add the eggs and bacon to the barbeque to have everything ready simultaneously and showed her how to dish up. The cowboys arrived in dribs and drabs, which helped immensely.

They lined up waiting for their food, and each of them welcomed her. Simone felt herself relax a little more now that breakfast was almost over.

"Once we stack the dishwasher, we'll get onto baking," Mrs Simpson explained once they were back in the kitchen.

It was going to be a long day.

* * *

After the day's baking was done, Mrs Simpson took her for a tour of the ranch.

Not the entire ranch – Mrs Simpson told her that would take literally days. No, she showed her the immediate area; places she needed to know about.

"This is the hen-house," she said. "Let them out in the morning and collect the eggs." She showed Simone all the hen's hiding places where she'd find them. "Lock them up after supper."

They went around the side of the house next. "This was Mrs Hadley's garden. Her pride and joy." She wiped a tear from her face. "We all loved the missus." She looked at Simone sternly. "You look after this veggie patch. Don't you let it die."

"I won't, I promise," Simone told her. She would do her upmost to keep it alive.

She motioned to her far right. "That's the chapel. It's always open – day and night. You go there whenever you want."

It looked very welcoming.

After Mrs Simpson left her, she wandered over to take a look.

The chapel was beautiful. It had either been well looked after or had been restored. The windows were all beautiful stained glass, in the style she'd come to expect in a chapel, and the pews all bore cushions.

She reached down and pulled out a bible, her hands covering it, as if drawing strength. In a way she was – she came here to pray for the strength to get her through. To ensure she learned from Mrs Simpson, and to do the best job she could.

The last thing she wanted was to leave. Everyone had been so welcoming and friendly. She hadn't come across that in a very long time.

She also prayed for her friend Amy. They'd lived in the same foster home for several years, practically grown up together, and Simone hadn't seen her for quite a while. She missed her friend. A lot.

She didn't know how long she'd been sitting there but was startled by a noise. She stood and turned toward the sound.

"Howdy, Ma'am," the cowboy said, taking his hat from his head. "I'm Joe, one of the cowpokes. Everyone calls me Old Joe." He grinned.

Simone figured he was in his late forties, or early fifties, so the name was probably more about how long he'd been there, than his age.

She extended her hand. "Pleased to meet you Joe. I'm Simone."

"I know." He grinned. "Hard to miss a pretty lady around here."

Simone felt the heat rise in her cheeks, and quickly headed toward the entrance.

"Miss Simone," he called after her. "If you have any trouble with any of the boys, you let me know, alright? I'll straighten them out."

She nodded and went out into the brisk Montana air.

* * *

"Something smells great!"

Mrs Simpson turned to Beau and glared. "What are you doing in here, Beau?"

He put his hands in the air and backed off. "Wondering how Simone is going, and making sure she's settled, is all."

"Thank you," Simone told him. "I appreciate it, but I think I'm doing okay. Mrs Simpson is a wonderful teacher."

Beau grinned. "Of course she is, and she's an amazing cook. What are you baking?"

"Blueberry muffins. I've never made this many before though." She looked toward the commercial size oven. "Never seen an oven as big as this one either."

"You'll get used to it."

And just like that he was gone.

"He's nice," Simone said.

"That he is lass, but mind you don't take too much of a liking to the young Hadley boys. I'm not sure Mr Hadley would be happy."

"I won't, I promise. I'm totally not interested. I just want to do my job."

"Good. That's settled then."

Simone glanced at her watch. "Twenty minutes until break. I'll get quicker, I promise."

"You're doing good, girly. Don't you stress it."

A few minutes later Nash Hadley wandered into the kitchen. "What is wrong with you boys today? Git out of my kitchen! Don't you have work to do?"

He smiled at Simone.

"Oh no you don't," Mrs Simpson said. "Go away. You boys are the absolute limit. Git!"

His smile disappeared, and he backed out in record time.

"Them boys are trying to get on with you, girly."

Simone was shocked. *Really?* Well she wasn't in the least interested. She needed this job and needed the money, *and* somewhere to live. She didn't need the grief of having a boyfriend. Especially not the boss's kid.

The timer on the oven brought her out of her thoughts. "Use the oven gloves," Mrs Simpson said. "They're much safer. The wooden block in the middle of the room is to put these trays on. Use it."

Simone nodded and followed her instructions. She'd been doing a lot of that lately.

"Morning." It was Vern this time. "Thought I'd pop my head in and see how your prodigy is going."

Mrs Simpson grinned. First time Simone had seen her smile all day. "She's doing well, Mr Hadley. Really well."

"After twenty-four years you still won't call me Vern." He shook his head. "Keep up the good work, Simone. And thank you, Mrs Simpson," he said, then left the room.

She lifted the first tray of large muffins out of the oven. "They smell good," she said.

"Test 'em. Make sure they're cooked." She was handed a skewer. "That's the exact time I bake them. Stick to that and you'll have perfect muffins every time."

Simone pulled the rest of the muffins out of the oven and placed them on a cooling rack. It was nearly time for the men to arrive.

Once cooled they were placed on trays and taken into the dining room. They topped up the coffee and sugar, made sure there were enough cups, plates and spoons, and waited for the dining room to fill up.

She felt his presence before she saw him. His unique fragrance filled her nostrils and the warmth of his body touched her in ways she'd never been touched before.

She felt the warmth of his fingers on her arm. The zing of it went through her like a rocket launching. "Am I allowed to get in early?"

She turned around to see him grinning. "Nope. Sorry. Mrs Simpson says I have to be tough. Especially with you Hadley boys." She couldn't help but laugh.

He met her eyes, and she couldn't pull hers away. He slowly leaned in to her.

"Simone, did you…" The words died on Mrs Simpson's lips. "Oh no you don't Beau Hadley. You leave my girl alone. I know what you boys are like."

She grabbed the kitchen towel from her waistband and flicked it at him. "Git."

He grinned at Simone and took off. She watched as he strolled toward the stables.

"Damned Hadley's. You keep that boy away." She turned and went back to the kitchen. It wasn't long after that the room filled. The muffins were quickly consumed, and it was time for the clean up once again.

Chapter Three

Simone was becoming quite good at baking.

Mrs Simpson wrote down all her recipes, since they were mostly in her head. Mr Hadley had ordered the older woman take the day off, as a dry run for Simone – to see how she coped on her own.

So far so good.

"What are you baking?"

She sighed. "Don't you ever work, Beau Hadley? You always seem to be in this kitchen." She grinned. She'd done her best impersonation of Mrs Simpson.

He laughed. She loved when he laughed. The little wrinkles around his eyes bunched up, and his face relaxed. His mouth opened wide, and his smile took up half the width of his face.

She was getting way too fond of him.

"You seem happy." He looked around. "Where's Mrs Simpson?"

Simone's smile disappeared. "I'm on my own today. Your father gave her the day off – to see how I fared."

She turned her back on him and returned to mixing the muffins. She added a little more flour but tipped it in too quickly and it went everywhere.

Beau laughed.

"It's not funny. Look at this mess!" It was everywhere – all over the benchtop, all over her apron, even flying through the air. It felt as though it was all over her face and in her hair.

He stepped toward her and his demeanor suddenly changed. Their eyes locked and Simone couldn't look away. Didn't want to look away.

His hand reached out and brushed the flour from her cheek. "Beau," she said, warning him to keep his distance.

"I'm so glad you came here, Simone," he said. "Every day has new meaning now. I look forward to getting up every day." He brushed at her other cheek. "You really are a mess," he said, his expression serious.

He leaned forward, his lips only an angel's breath away. Simone continued to stare into his eyes. "Tell me no and I'll back off," he said quietly.

She stayed silent. It was only the lightest of kisses, but when his lips touched hers, Simone's heart sang. She leaned into him and rested her head on his shoulder.

"I really like you, Beau," she said softly.

"I really like you too, Simone. More than like."

They were so engrossed in each other they didn't hear Mrs Simpson come into the kitchen. "Beau Hadley, get your hands off my girl," she said quietly.

* * *

Simone was exhausted. She'd been on the Silver Shoe Ranch for nearly a week now but hadn't had time to sit and rest.

She was getting better at what she had to do, and Mrs Simpson was a Godsend. She had no idea what she would do without the older lady there to guide her.

She'd learned an awful lot in a relatively short period of time, and only had her assistance for another few weeks at most.

Vern, Mr Hadley, had already spoken to her about catering a small party to celebrate Mrs Simpson's retirement.

This would be all up to her, because it was to be a surprise. She took a deep breath. It would be a challenge, but she was certain she could pull it off.

She wouldn't have said that a week ago.

"You must be freezing."

She looked up to see Beau standing nearby with a blanket in his hands. She'd been sitting out on the porch watching the sunset.

She'd never done that in the city.

Not that it was the same, because it wasn't. Out here, in the middle of nowhere, the sun was huge. The horizon seemed much closer, and the sun moving down below it much larger.

You got to experience the clouds moving across the sky. And you got to enjoy the peace and quiet.

She pulled her cardigan further around her shoulders. "I guess I am. I've been watching the sunset. It's the most beautiful thing I've ever seen."

"It certainly is beautiful." He pulled a blanket around her shoulders and tucked her in tight. "You're not used to Montana weather, are you?" She heard the curiosity in his voice.

"I'm from interstate," she said quickly, hoping he'd move on. She wasn't interested in telling anyone her life story. And he probably didn't want to hear it.

"It's going to get colder, the closer we get to Christmas. I hope you have warm clothing," he said, but the question was clearly heard.

She gazed up at him and shook her head. "I didn't bring much with me. I figured I'd be indoors most of the time." The truth of the matter was, all her worldly possessions were in that bag, and all she had were a few changes of clothes.

"I'll take you into town once you're settled."

"No!" The thought terrified her. "I mean, uh, the truth is, I don't have any money until I'm paid."

She watched his thoughts ticking over. Then the realization that hit him.

He sat next to her and spoke quietly. "You're working for us, and only need that gear because you're here." He stared into her face as though he was trying to understand her better. "The ranch will pay for whatever you need."

"Please no. I don't want to be a burden." She turned her head away so he couldn't see how upset she was. "Besides, I don't have time. I have very full days."

"We'll go Friday. I'm sure Mrs Simpson won't mind taking over the baking for the day. There, no excuses."

"But,"

"We'll leave at nine-thirty. It's a long drive into town."

He stood then, leaving Simone to her own thoughts. Thoughts like how she would survive in a car with Beau in such close proximity for the long drive.

She brushed it aside for now and sat back to enjoy the panoramic view in front of her. It was thoughtful of Beau to bring her a blanket. It didn't even enter her mind to grab one.

Her mind drifted off, and she was having a lovely dream; one of living on this ranch for many years to come, like Mrs Simpson. Of being appreciated, and perhaps even loved. Something she hadn't experienced since her parents had died.

She dreamed of familiar faces and her own bed, one that she slept in every night forever.

Her eyes fluttered open and she looked up to see Beau leaning over her. "It's alright," he whispered. "Go back to sleep." He kissed her forehead gently.

She was in her own room. She'd fallen asleep on the porch, and he'd carried her in.

It was just like Beau – he was thoughtful in every way.

She rolled over and he pulled the blanket over her, then slipped quietly out of the room. She dreamed of Beau, of kissing him, and being in his arms. Even in her sleep-filled state, she knew she shouldn't.

* * *

Beau was excited.

It was Friday and he was taking Simone into Hidden Valley to do some shopping. It would be a good chance to get to know her better as well.

Mrs Simpson was taking over the baking for the day. Simone refused to come with him unless she prepared breakfast, so that was the compromise.

Mrs Simpson said she was bored now, since Simone is doing most of the work. She'd picked everything up very quickly.

"Go Simone, and don't worry about anything. Remember what I said about Beau." It was Mrs Simpson's voice. "Don't get too close."

He was annoyed. Mrs Simpson had her reasons for keeping them apart, but that didn't make him feel any better.

It was true they'd spent many months trying to get a new cook. Simone was the only one who'd answered the advert.

But he wasn't going to let that stand in the way. He had feelings for her, and he hoped she felt the same way.

He suddenly stiffened. What if she didn't and she was only humoring him to keep her job? The thought had never occurred to him before.

Perhaps that's why Mrs Simpson was pushing them apart. She might know something he didn't.

He frowned.

Was that the case? Was he making a fool of himself?

"I'm finally ready!" He glanced up to see her smiling face and all his doubts disappeared. For now.

He looked her up and down. Her get-up only reinforced the need for warmer clothes. "Great. Let's get going then. It's a long drive."

She wore flimsy summer-weight denims with a cotton button-through shirt. Over it she wore a light cardigan.

She had trainers on her feet – at least that was a plus.

He opened the door to her, and she frowned. "You don't have to open the door you know. I am quite capable…"

"So am I. You're not used to being looked after, are you?" She cringed. "I'm sorry. Forget I said anything."

He saw her looking around as they navigated the long drive from the ranch to the *main* road, which wasn't much better than a dirt road.

"Oh, of course," he suddenly said. "You arrived in the dark."

"It's really beautiful," she said quietly. "How much of this is your family's property?" She continued to look around.

"All of it. We own all the land for as far as you can see, and then some."

Her eyes opened wide. "Seriously?"

"Ever ridden a horse?" He glanced across at her momentarily, keeping his eyes on the road.

She laughed. The sound of it lifted his heart. "You're kidding, right? I've never seen a real horse, let alone ridden one."

He couldn't believe what he was hearing. But he should. He'd heard of this before – city people having no contact with farm animals.

Beau felt sad for her. "We'll work on changing that," he said.

She nodded and continued her perusal of the area while he drove.

Somewhere along the way Simone had nodded off. It was a long day when you weren't used to it, but she was getting there, he was certain.

He lightly shook her shoulder. "We're here." No response. "Simone?" A little more loudly this time.

Her eyes fluttered open. "Hmmm?"

"I must have fallen asleep. Is this it? Hidden Valley?"

"Sure is. We'll take a quick wander to stretch our legs, then get some lunch before we go shopping. Is that okay with you?"

She stifled a yawn. "Whatever works." She let her hair down and began to put it back into a pony tail. He reached out and touched her hand.

"Leave it out? I never get to see you with your hair down."

"It's a mess. It has to be."

He stared at her. "It's not a mess. You're beautiful." He suddenly pulled back and stopped the car. He could easily sit there with her all day, but it would be a trap. He'd want to stay put, with her in his arms.

Beau showed her around town. Not that there was much to see, but it was all they had without traveling a lot further to the city. If they did that, they flew in the ranch plane.

"Not much choice for lunch, I'm afraid." He pointed to a couple of buildings. "The hotel or the diner. They're both good."

She nodded but didn't answer.

"You choose," he told her.

"I, uh," She looked bewildered. "Beau, I don't have any money for lunch," she finally said.

He frowned. Didn't he make it clear he was paying? "It's my treat. Along with the clothes. Now you choose. Please?"

Not for the first time he wondered about her situation. He'd fully intended to pay for her, no question. But why was she so flat broke?

He shook his head. *Nope. Wasn't his business.*

He hooked his arm through hers and stared into her pretty face. "Which way?"

Chapter Four

"I can't eat another thing."

Beau laughed. He loved to see her happy, and right now she was happy and very relaxed. He couldn't begin to imagine the stress she'd been under at the ranch.

She'd been thrown in the deep end. He was certain she hadn't known what she was getting into when she answered that advert.

From his perspective, he had no idea she would need so much training. His father had discussed the position with his sons when her letter arrived. After all, it affected them too.

Reading between the lines they should have realized she had no experience, but with no other applicants, they had to take the chance.

"Coffee?" The waitress was standing over him waiting for an answer.

"Sorry. Yes please. For two?" He looked across at Simone and watched as she cringed. She was still worried about the cost. "My shout, remember? Coffee for two, thanks."

"Tell me about the ranch." She seemed keen to know, but he wondered if it was just a ploy to change the subject.

"Where do I start? I guess at the beginning. It has been in family hands for over a hundred years. The ranch itself has been restored over the years. It was a pretty awful mess at one stage."

"I know you employ a lot of people," she said. "But what do they all do?" Heat crept up her face. He wasn't sure why she was embarrassed to ask, but the pink flushes in her cheeks suited her. She was way too pale for his liking.

"We're a cattle ranch. We have a few thousand head. Okay, maybe more." His mouth twitched as he tried not to grin. It was definitely a lot more.

"But, I,"

"Haven't seen any cattle?"

She nodded.

"That's because they're in the back paddocks at the moment. We rotate the paddocks they're in regularly. Next month they'll be closer in, and you'll likely see them."

"What about the horses?"

He wondered when she would ask. "Purely work horses. There was a time we bred them, but that's seriously hard work with no guarantees, so we stick with cattle now."

The waitress returned with their coffees. "Can I get you anything else, Sir?"

Beau looked up at the waitress, then across to Simone who shook her head.

"No, I think we're done for now. Thank you."

He lifted his coffee to his lips.

"I have an idea," he suddenly said. "Since you've never met a horse, let's say I introduce you to one?" He reached across and covered her hand with his.

"I don't know…"

"Don't be scared. I'll hook you up with one of the more placid mares." He squeezed her hand. "It's a date then – Sunday after breakfast."

She didn't look too sure, but Beau would help her through it. "Drink up, and then we're off to do some shopping."

It wasn't his favorite thing to do, but Simone needed to be kitted out with decent weather-proof clothes, and he was there to see she was.

* * *

"I, I can't."

They stood at the shop counter while the assistant rang up the purchases. This was a store Beau used regularly – they stocked everything from cotton shirts, to thick pullovers, to boots, to snow gear.

The pile was high, and there were already three large bags worth, with more yet to be filled.

"You can, and you will." Beau pulled out his wallet and flashed his plastic. "It's a done deal." He winked at the assistant who was carefully watching their exchange.

She was fighting a losing battle, and was finally beginning to give in. He leaned forward and whispered to the sales assistant. "Do me a favor and don't mention the total."

She nodded. "My friend is very upset about me buying this stuff for her, so…"

"Oh. Sure."

Simone stood in the doorway, moving from one foot to the other. Her nerves getting the better of her.

He struggled to carry the five bags and passed one over to Simone. "It's too much, Beau," she said. "I'll pay you back, I promise."

"You won't you know. I won't let you." Now he was getting annoyed. Why couldn't she just accept his gifts and move on.

And then it hit him. She was too proud. She'd obviously been in a bad situation and had to fend for herself for a very long time.

"We can talk about that some other time." That seemed to cheer her up, which made him happy.

After placing the bags in the 4x4 he grabbed her hand and guided her toward another store. "Here's my plastic. Get yourself some, um, delicates and um, unmentionable, er, lady stuff." He felt the heat crawl up his face. "Whatever you need. I'll wait here."

Simone's face went beet red.

"We don't come into town very often, so make sure you get plenty." He started to walk away. "I'll be across the road at the park. Call my cell if you need me."

"I can't, Beau."

"You can. If you won't go in alone, I'll come with you."

She shook her head. He watched as she walked into the store and headed toward the back.

Twenty minutes later she resurfaced with three bags of goodies. "All done?"

"All done." She handed over the credit card, along with the receipt. "Keep it. I don't need to know what you bought." He smiled and watched as the tension left her face.

"Unless there's anything else you need, we'll head back to the ranch." She reached out and took his hand. Despite the cool afternoon air, her hand was warm. And small.

He wanted to hold her, not just her hand. He wanted to protect her and keep her safe forever. He'd never felt like this before.

Mrs Simpson told him it was because they don't see many women way out there in Grand Falls, but he knew better.

She was totally wrong.

There was something about Simone. He felt a real connection to her. He sensed it the first time he met her.

When he was working, his thoughts would turn to her. His concentration wasn't like it used to be. Little things reminded him of her. The lavender in the garden reminded him of her perfume. The sunlight reminded him of her eyes.

And the aroma that drifted out from the kitchen was a constant reminder.

"Thank you, Beau," she said when they were on their way home. "No one has ever done anything like that for me before."

He reached across and squeezed her hand. "You are very welcome." He let go of her hand and concentrated on the road. "Maybe tonight we can watch the sunset together. You'll be able to endure the cold now."

"I'd like that. I really would."

Simone's cell phone rang. "Amy? Is that you? You'll never guess where I am!"

Beau concentrated on the road and zoned out while Simone talked to her caller. A friend perhaps? He couldn't wait for sunset. He'd love nothing more than to sit with Simone and watch the day end.

* * *

Simone couldn't believe how much stuff Beau had bought for her. It must have cost a fortune. She felt really bad, because he wouldn't let her pay him back, despite what he said in town. She also knew arguing about it was futile.

Her day was now done, and it wouldn't be long before the sun began to set.

She'd put most of her new clothes, her warm clothes, away in the wardrobe, but pulled a thick pullover over her head. It was so warm and cozy, and she stared at herself in the mirror.

It was really pretty.

She knew Beau liked it; he'd worn a big grin when he saw her wearing it in the store. It also had a big price tag and she'd tried to put it back on the shelf.

He'd snatched it from her and given it to the sales assistant to put aside.

She pulled on the thick woolen socks and cowboy boots he'd bought for her and dragged the gloves onto her hands. Last of all she pushed her arms into the snow jacket.

It was so snuggly and warm.

She didn't think she would need the beanie but shoved it into a pocket in the jacket anyway.

He was already waiting on the porch when she arrived. Two hot beverages sat on the low table used for that very purpose.

She headed for the chair right outside the door. "Come over here," he told her. "Next to me. You're too far away over there."

She moved but wasn't certain it was a good idea. They were getting far too close already.

"The gear looks good," he told her, pulling his own jacket around himself.

She zipped up the jacket against the cold. "It's lovely and warm. Thank you again. I can't believe the difference it makes."

She sat, and he handed her a mug of hot coffee. Despite the thick gloves covering her hands, she felt a tingle when their hands brushed. His eyes shot up and stared into her face.

"I know you've only been here for a short time," he began. "But I have feelings for you, Simone."

She glared at him. "No you don't," she said quietly. "You can't. Not this soon. It's like Mrs Simpson said, you just think you do."

But what if he did? She was starting to have feelings for him too. She sighed. The end of her trial period was closing in on her. She hoped Mr Hadley let her stay.

She had no idea what she would do, or where she would go, if he didn't. Not to mention her feelings for Beau.

He reached across and held one of her hands in his. "I don't care what Mrs Simpson says," he told her, still holding her hand. "She can't know how I feel."

Simone reluctantly pulled her hand away and rested it in her lap. His eyes burned her.

She watched the sun go slowly down and reveled in the fact Beau was there with her.

Tonight, she wasn't alone. But what about in a week's time? Or even a month? She could be banished from this place.

This beautiful place that truly felt like home.

* * *

Beau chose the quietest horse in the stables.

Blaze was a five-year-old Palomino with a white blaze running from her forehead, almost to the tip of her nose.

She was born on the ranch and would live her life out there. "Hello, Blaze." He held his hand out for her to get used to his smell, then pulled a piece of carrot out of his pocket.

She greedily gobbled it up, then rubbed her head against his shoulder.

"Give me your hand." He knew Simone would be nervous, so was taking it easy. He slowly pulled her hand toward the laid-back mare.

He felt her stiffen. "She won't bite, will she?"

He laughed. "Blaze, bite? Never." He continued to pull her hand to the horse's face. "Let her sniff you, then you can give her some carrot."

Simone nodded and relaxed a little. Blaze brushed her teeth across her trembling hand. She quickly pulled her hand back.

Beau grabbed her hand. "Don't stress. She's just searching for more carrot. Shall we try again?"

He could see how terrified she was of the horse. It was obvious she'd had little exposure to animals throughout her life.

Simone nodded, very unenthusiastically. He wondered if he was pushing her too hard. She took a deep breath, and he could see she was psyching herself up to do this.

Atta girl!

He placed her hand in his, both cupped ready for the carrot. "We'll go more slowly this time," he said. "I shouldn't have pushed you."

He reached out with the other hand and rubbed the horse's back. She leaned in toward Simone's hand and the carrot and sniffed. Then she swooped on the piece of carrot, gobbling it up quickly.

Her head suddenly went down looking for more. Simone jumped back, scaring Blaze who whinnied, then quickly stepped back.

Beau saw the terrified expression on Simone's face. "It's fine, she's fine. You gave her a fright, that's all." He grinned knowing that was exactly what the horse had done to Simone.

He opened the door to Blaze's stall, reins in hand.

"What are you doing?" She looked downright terrified.

He looped the reins over the horse's head and began to lead her out. "We'll just go for a short stroll around the paddock with her. You can get to know each other better."

He reached into his pocket and pulled out some apple this time. "Here, give her this." He watched as Simone's expression changed. A moment ago, she was terrified, now she was deciding if it was worth the risk.

She reached out and offered the cut-up apple, even stroking the horses face.

They walked slowly but surely around the paddock, Beau holding the reins. "Here, you take over. Walk slowly, but steadily. Talk to her gently as you go."

He thrust the reins into Simone's hands, not giving her a choice. She frowned.

"You *can* do this."

And she did. They walked around the small paddock twice. He was surprised at how well she'd managed her first time. Blaze was a big part of that familiarization, which was the reason he chose her. He needed a calm and quiet mare, and that she was.

It was a bitter-sweet moment, since Blaze had been his mother's horse. No one wanted to ride her, to honor their mother, but she needed to be exercised. He dutifully walked her every day, then let her run, but it wasn't the same.

He hoped he could eventually convince Simone to ride her. Blaze deserved as much.

He closed his eyes against the emotions forcing their way out. It had been nearly a year since Marianne Hadley had died but it seemed like only yesterday.

The family were still trying to come to terms with her sudden death.

Blaze whinnied and rubbed her head against Simone's shoulder. "She likes you," he said quietly. "I'll take the reins off and she can have a run for a while."

The horse took off in a trot, then moved into a canter, running from one end of the paddock to the other. She finally came to rest next to Simone, rubbing her head against her shoulder, then sniffing her hand.

For the first time since they started this adventure, Simone smiled.

"She really likes you," Beau told her.

"I like her too," she said. "A lot."

He hoped this was the beginning of a long relationship between the pair.

Chapter Five

"Ready?"

Beau was more than a little enthusiastic this morning. "Almost."

Simone removed her apron and carried the cut-up banana bread out to the dining room. The urn was hot, and everything else was ready.

"Now I'm ready." She was excited about seeing Blaze again. She was such a sweet and gentle horse. Not that she had any idea whether that was normal.

"You'll need your jacket," Beau said. "It's pretty cold out this morning. Won't be long and the snow will come."

"You're kidding, right? It doesn't snow here does it?" She knew she was frowning, but she couldn't help it.

"Closer to Christmas. We always enjoy a white Christmas here in Grand Falls. You just wait and see – you'll love it too."

She shrugged on the thick jacket and her gloves. "I might not be here," she said quietly, still unaware if her position was secured.

Beau stared at her for long moments. "You'll be here, I'm certain," he said, as he helped her into the warm jacket.

"Forget about that. Let's go."

Blaze was standing in her stall looking at them and whinnied. It was almost as if she'd been waiting for them. "Hello Blaze," Simone said, extending her hand. Blaze took the offered carrot, then looked for more.

Beau stared at her. "You're pretty game today."

"You told me she won't bite, and she was perfect yesterday."

He grabbed the reins and entered the stall. "Did you want to do this today?"

Simone shook her head. "Not today, but I'll watch, if that's okay. Maybe I'll try another time."

He offered her the reins once they were on the horse, and she took them. Yesterday was such a positive experience, and she hoped today would be the same.

She strolled through the stables, head held high, as if to say, *look at me, I'm leading a horse!* Blaze shoved her shoulder, but Simone continued to walk toward the small paddock they'd used previously.

She didn't ask Beau for instructions, just followed yesterday's lead. Blaze followed her around until Simone attempted to remove the reins. She couldn't work it out and felt deflated.

"It's easy, once you know how," Beau told her. She nodded and watched, then he let her do it. Blaze took off in a trot, then moved into a canter.

"She loves running about," she said.

Beau stared at the horse running around, enjoying herself immensely. "She does," he said quietly. "I'm afraid she's been neglected for way too long."

Simone stared at him, not saying a word.

He straightened his shoulders and continued to stare at the horse. "She was my mother's horse. No one has ridden her since she died nearly a year ago."

"I'm so sorry," Simone said, then moved in and hugged him. His arms came up around her.

She was supposed to be comforting him, but she felt comfortable in his arms. Her head resting on his shoulder, she felt as though this was where she was meant to be.

"Don't let Mrs Simpson see you," Beau quipped.

Simone laughed. "She might flick her kitchen towel at you again!"

She pushed back and gazed into his face. He looked contented. More content than she'd seen him since she arrived.

He was smiling too. He didn't do that often. He seemed to absorb himself in his work, and not much more. He only let his guard down at night when the family sat around the fire. She'd been invited to spend her time with them, but most of the time, she refused.

She didn't want to intrude.

She moved to the fence and stared out across the range. "It's so beautiful here," she said. "I could take in this view forever."

"I hope you do," Beau said, as he slipped his arm around her shoulders.

She sighed. "I guess it's up to your father. I've been here for quite a few weeks now, and he hasn't said anything to me. My trial time must just about be up."

He squeezed her shoulders. "I'm certain you'll be fine." He turned to face her. "Do you like it here, Simone?" he asked. He'd never asked the question before.

She didn't hesitate. "I love it. It feels like home, and everyone is so nice." She didn't dare tell him she'd never had a real home. Moving from foster home to foster home most of her childhood after her parents died in a plane crash, had totally ruined her life. At least in her eyes.

When she turned eighteen, she was let loose to fend for herself. That hadn't worked out so well, and she'd been living basically homeless ever since.

Her rundown car was her main possession, and even that was pretty terrible.

"I love my room too," she said. "Even if I do have to close the curtains when I'm dressing." She laughed, and Beau pulled her in for another hug.

"I love that you like it here," he whispered. "I'm so glad we met."

She closed her eyes and reveled in his nearness. She didn't want to move out of his arms, but she had to. They had a visitor – Blaze was pushing her face between them, wanting to get in on the action.

They both laughed at her antics. "Can she stay out here all day," Simone asked.

He rubbed his hands over the animals back. "Afraid not. It's way to cold. She needs to go back in now." He lifted the reins. "Want to give it a try?"

She was eager to try and knew Beau would help her if needed.

She lifted the reins, showing Blaze what she was about to do, as Beau had instructed her. She slipped them on and began to lead the horse back into the stables.

"You two were meant for each other," Beau said quietly. "My mother would be so happy."

* * *

Simone finished plaiting her blonde hair, then shrugged on her sweater, and finally her jacket.

She took a deep breath.

Today she was going to have her first horse-riding lesson.

Beau would meet her at the stables, which meant she'd have time to spend with Blaze.

The walk to the stables seemed to take forever without him at her side. She pulled her jacket around herself against the icy cold Montana weather.

Blazed whinnied as she approached, and Simone reached into her deep pockets and pulled out pieces of apple.

The horse rubbed her head against Simone's shoulder, then the side of her face.

"Hello girl," Simone said quietly, not wanting to startle her. Blaze whinnied again and was rewarded with more apple.

Feeling a little more game, she reached for the reins and entered the stall. She would walk the horse out to the paddock, ready for Beau when he arrived.

He had an early start but would be back soon.

Blaze didn't seem to mind.

The reins securely in place, they walked outside. She began to follow their usual pattern when he arrived.

Simone stopped where she was and stared. Stared at the cowboy standing in front of her. Her heart began to race. She'd never seen him atop his horse, and it set her on fire.

This was a different Beau to the one she'd seen before. She'd seen him in his cowboy outfit, and even seen him with his cowboy hat. But atop a horse was a whole new perspective.

Whoa!

She fanned her face despite the nip in the air.

He smiled a slow smile. "You're being adventurous." He nodded in the direction of Blaze.

Phew! She thought he'd read her mind. "I've done it enough times now, I can manage." She wasn't so sure about the riding part though.

"Let me fix Storm up and I'll be back." He dismounted the horse and led him into the stables. His stall was next to Blaze's stall, but Simone knew once he'd rested, Beau would let him into the paddocks.

She continued to walk the horse, and finally took her back to the stables, only to see Beau brushing his horse down lovingly.

She knew how much Blaze enjoyed a good brushing, and it was clear Storm did too.

When he was done, Storm took himself into his stall ready for a feed.

"Right. Time to saddle up your horse." Her horse? Until now she'd been his mother's horse. Her heart beat triple time. "She's not my horse," she said quietly. "Blaze will always be your mother's horse."

He shook his head, but Simone was certain he knew in his heart she was right.

He put the saddle blanket on, then the saddle. Was it the same saddle his mother used, Simone wondered?

He reached for a riding helmet, and they left the stables. "We'll stick to the paddock today," he said. "When you feel more confident, we'll venture further out."

She swallowed. Further out? How far further out? The Silver Shoe Ranch was huge.

"Put your left foot in the stirrup," he said, putting the reins in her hands. "And grab hold of the saddle horn. That's it. Now swing your other leg up and over."

She stared at him. Was he for real? That sounded impossible.

She gave it a go, and almost landed on her butt. He grabbed her before she hit the ground.

He stood laughing at her.

"It's not funny," she said half heartedly, her hands on her hips.

"It really is. Try again," he said more seriously.

"That's it. Do a little bounce as you put your second leg over." She looked at him as though he was crazy. "Seriously. It helps."

He grabbed hold of her hips to help her over. Warmth spread through her, and she lost her concentration, falling sideways, right into his arms.

He wrapped them around her. "Simone…"

She looked up into his face, and he lifted his hand, touching her cheek. His head slowly moved toward hers until their mouths were only an angel's wings apart. She could taste his breath, he was so close.

"Beau, I…"

He lightly brushed her lips with his own. His hands went up around her back. She moved closer, and his lips covered hers.

She leaned into him, then as their lips separated, she rested her head on his shoulder. It felt good there, the warmth of his body warming hers despite the cold.

All thought left her. All she wanted to do was stand there with Beau. The world around them disappeared. There was peace and quiet, nothing was going to interrupt their time together.

Suddenly, Blaze whinnied, and they jumped apart.

Simone looked up into his face. His eyes burned into her, and her heart beat increased once again.

"Ready to try again," he said, as though nothing had happened between them.

She heard laughter in the near distance and spun her head in that direction. Sitting on the paddock fence were several of the cowboys – how much had they seen?

She felt the color creep up her face. "Maybe we should give up today?" She knew that was not Beau's way, but she felt incredibly embarrassed. Especially if they had seen everything. That kiss. She felt flushed just thinking about it.

He took the reins from her. "Nope. No way." He stood beside Blaze. "Watch carefully. This is how you mount a horse."

She watched as his foot went into the stirrup, as he grabbed the saddle horn, while holding the reins. "Watch this other leg. This is the important bit."

She stepped back to get a good look. In one swift movement, Beau was atop the horse. Then just as quickly he was off again.

"Now you try it."

It seemed easy enough.

She stepped forward and took the reins from him. She talked gently to Blaze before attempting to mount her again.

Beau held her hips again. Heat surged through her. "You can let go. I won't fall," she said. But what she really meant was 'you do things to me'.

He dropped his hands quickly, and she let out the breath she'd been holding.

Before she realized, she was sitting upright in the saddle, atop her horse.

"Well done!" Beau was smiling broadly, and she couldn't help herself – she was smiling too.

Her hands were sweating inside the thick gloves, but not from the warmth. She was sitting on a horse – on Blaze. Oh my.

"Are you ready to ride her?" He stared at her, waiting for her answer.

She shook her head. "Okay. We'll take it easy today then." She breathed a sigh of relief. "Give me the reins and I'll walk you around the paddock. Tomorrow though, you ride properly."

Simone bit her lip. She wasn't sure if she was ready for that. She passed over the reins, and Beau moved forward. Blaze automatically followed him.

"Mother loved this horse," he said quietly. "I can see you love her too. She can be cantankerous and doesn't let just anyone ride her."

He looked back at her. "You're one of the chosen few."

Simone was surprised. "I haven't seen her like that."

"That's because she likes you."

She looked up to see Mr Hadley standing at the edge of the stables, motioning for them to come in.

"Ooops, I guess our time is up," she said. "Now how do I get off?"

* * *

Mr Hadley sat at his big desk in the study.

Simone sat opposite him, Beau leaning against the back wall. She was certain she was about to be sacked, and asked Beau to come in with her.

"You don't need to be here, Beau," he said, glaring at his son.

Beau smiled. "You're scary, Dad. I'm her moral support."

Mr Hadley did not look impressed.

"Alright," he said abruptly. "Let's get on with it then." He shuffled some papers around his desk, then stared at Simone.

"You've been here a while now," he said, more gently this time. "How are you finding it?"

She was taken aback and wasn't sure how to answer. "I, uh," She licked her lips. Her mouth was suddenly dry. "I like it," she finally got out. "I love the peace and quiet. I don't particularly like the early mornings, but the rest is good."

He leaned back in his chair. Beau put his hand to her shoulder, as though warning her to brace herself.

Mr Hadley cleared his throat. "The job is yours if you want it," he said abruptly.

Simone was certain she'd heard wrong. "When do you want me to leave, Mr Hadley?" she asked, tears welling up in her eyes. "I," She didn't know when it had happened, but this place had become home. Her real home, and now she had to leave. A tear rolled down her cheek.

Beau squeezed her shoulder. "You're not leaving," he said, a smile on his face.

"The job is yours, Simone," Mr Hadley said again. "And for goodness sakes, call me Vern."

"Thank you, Mr Hadley. Er, Vern," she said, her voice breaking.

"Mrs Simpson has taught you well. You're an excellent cook, and the boys all love what you bake." He motioned to the door. "Now go and enjoy the rest of your day off. Tomorrow is one of those early starts you hate so much." He grinned, and Simone realized he was joking with her.

Beau pulled her to her feet and brushed his lips across hers.

"Get a room," Vern said. "On second thoughts, don't. It's taken forever to get someone to come all the way out here. I don't want to lose her."

Beau laughed and pulled her out of Vern's study.

"Another riding lesson to celebrate?"

"No, I think I've had enough for today." She headed toward the kitchen. She felt like doing some baking – one of her favorite things to do.

Chapter Six

Against her better judgement, Beau had convinced her to go for a ride.

A real ride this time, not just a stroll around a paddock. She'd done all her chores for the morning and waited in the stables for him.

She was getting braver as time went on, and even put the reins on Blaze. Then she gave her a brush down. Blaze seemed to enjoy it.

"Ah, spoiling the horse, eh?" Beau's voice broke into her thoughts. He dismounted, then brushed Storm down, and moved him into his stall. "He's worked hard today. We've been fixing fences up in the back paddock.

Simone felt deflated. "He's probably too tired to ride then." She'd been looking forward to today, despite her anxiety.

Beau waved her concerns aside. "I'll be riding Jock. Storm has worked pretty hard today. He won't be happy, but he needs to rest."

Blaze stepped forward and shoved at his shoulder. "Hello girl," he said. "You're going to have a ball. Your first time out of the front paddock for nearly a year."

"I've packed a lunch, as well as a few muffins."

Beau brightened up. "Can't wait."

Simone had no idea where they were going, but it would be her first real ride. Out into the open that was.

"Saddle her up," he instructed, and reached for a saddle. "Do you remember how?"

She bit her bottom lip. "I think so. Maybe." She shook her head. "I'm not sure."

Beau stood beside her. "Go ahead and I'll watch. I don't want to risk you falling off."

He stood silently and watched as she nervously saddled the mare. "That's great. Just tighten the cinch a little more, so there's not so much movement."

She did as he said, seeing her mistake.

"Perfect. Grab the helmet and you're ready to go."

They left the moment Jock was saddled. Beau grabbed some bottled water from the refrigerator in the stables and put it in his saddle bags.

"Let's go."

Simone followed him, and they headed out. She had no idea where they were going but was sure it wouldn't be too far away. This was very new to her.

They'd been traveling less than half an hour when Beau brought Jock to a halt. "This is a spot where we used to have family picnics. It's a bit over-run now but will work for us today."

She nodded.

"You don't want to ride too far your first time." He patted his backside. "Gets a little tender until you're used to riding," he said, grinning.

"You can dismount now," he said as he climbed down from Jock's back.

Simone stared at him. "I'm scared," she said bluntly.

He grinned at her and was quickly by her side. He put his hands to her waist and she felt warmth fill her body.

"Okay, down you come."

As she dismounted, he held tightly to her waist. They suddenly came face to face. Closer than Simone anticipated. She felt his breath against her mouth as she leaned over to dismount. He lifted her off and leaned in slowly.

His hands slid around he waist and he pulled her closer. Their lips met in an explosion of stars. His breath was ragged and so was hers.

She'd never felt this way before. About anyone.

She quickly pulled back and rested her head on his shoulder. She had feelings for Beau that she knew she shouldn't have.

He was the boss's son, and she had no right to fall for him. But it was too late. Her heart was leading her head instead of the other way around.

She put her hands to his chest and pushed herself away. "I'd better organise the food," she said, busying herself with the task.

She'd even brought along a small blanket to lay on the ground.

Beau grinned at her, as though he knew what she was doing. Avoiding the fact they were falling in love.

Correction: had already fallen in love.

She'd only been there a little over a month, and her life had changed forever. Not only because of the wonderful gig she'd landed, but because of this wonderfully caring and loving man she'd met.

What if it didn't last and they broke up? What then?

She clutched at her chest. She suddenly felt hollow. Her head was spinning, and she slipped sideways. Beau was there to catch her.

"Whoa – are you alright?" He held her close to him.

She couldn't tell him about the heartbreak she'd anticipated. "I, uh, I'm okay now. I must have stood up too quickly."

"Or maybe you're hungry. Let's sit down and eat."

At least he'd accepted her explanation without question. Even come up with a good reason of his own.

She stared across at him as he ate. She'd never known how sexy a cowboy could be until she met Beau. His brothers didn't do a thing for her, not that she had seen much of them, they were always busy. So it wasn't the cowboy rep, it was the man himself.

"Man, you're a good cook," he suddenly declared. "These muffins are to die for." He took another mouthful. "A man could easily get used to this."

She watched as he chewed his food. How that simple act became sensual, she'd never know, but right now she wanted to kiss him.

She leaned forward and covered his lips with her own.

He didn't object. "Well, little lady," he said between kisses. "I didn't expect this."

She pulled back. "Sorry," she said quietly. "I, I overstepped the mark."

"Uh, uh. You most certainly did not." He grinned, her favorite way for him to be. His dimples made him look even more cute than he was already.

Cute in a manly way of course. He'd hate for her to think otherwise.

He held her tight as they lay on the blanket, staring up at the sky. Her head rested on his chest, and she could hear his heart beating wildly.

"Did you enjoy the ride?" he asked, tightening his hold on her.

"I did. Surprisingly."

He looked down at her. "I'm sure Blaze did too. She seemed happy to be out of that paddock."

Beau checked his watch. "As much as I'm enjoying being here with you, we'd better make a move."

She was disappointed but began to get up. "Good idea. I don't want to have to rush for tonight's supper."

He held her hands and helped Simone to her feet. Warmth flooded her.

Both horses trotted over to them when Beau called them, and they were soon on their way back to the ranch.

* * *

Simone had worked hard all day preparing for this night.

She had gone above and beyond to bake and keep everything a secret, knowing it meant a lot to Vern, as well as Mrs Simpson.

Yesterday had officially been her last day, so Simone had been able to prepare for the party without interruption.

Despite it being a celebration, it was also a somber time for some. After more than twenty years on the ranch, she was leaving.

Beau, more than anyone, knew how isolating it could be way out there on Silver Shoe Ranch. They were hours from anywhere. Anyone.

As a small child, it didn't bother him so much. There was always something to explore, and places to discover.

Many of the ranch hands were like a big brother to him. They took him in hand and taught him everything he knew now. As an adult, he loved the life, but not the isolation so much.

Despite having ranch hands, the Hadley boys all pitched in and did the hard work, just like the rest of the cowboys. That way they always knew what was going on and kept their skills up to date.

Vern did most of the paperwork, but the boys also had a hand in it. They were expected to take over the ranch one day, and paperwork was part of the job.

As the eldest Hadley, Beau would have to take on the majority of the paperwork.

"I'd like to thank Mrs Simpson for all her years of hard work feeding this mob," Vern motioned to the crowd in the dining room. The place won't be the same without her."

There was whistling and applauding. "I'd also like to thank Simone for the wonderful spread she's provided tonight. You did a great job, Simone." Vern smiled at her.

Now that Simone knew she was staying, she seemed more relaxed.

She did a little mock bow. She really had put on a wonderful spread. Not only did she bake muffins, cakes and slices, she made sausage rolls, little pies, quiches, cheese twists, corn dip, roasted parmesan potatoes, and various other savory treats.

She certainly was a trooper, which was just one of the reasons he'd come to love her.

There was so much to hate about this place – the isolation, the number of people she had to cook for, and not least, the cold. It was clear she wasn't used to it.

Beau wondered what she would think when the cold really set in. It was the one thing she complained about.

He hadn't yet told her it would be snowing for Christmas.

The speeches were over, and Vern handed a gift to Mrs Simpson as an appreciation of all she'd done. "There's a bonus in your pay this week too," he told her quietly, so only Beau could hear. He happened to know it was the equivalent of a month's pay.

Simone strolled past, and he pulled her to him. "I know this sounds horrible," he said so only she could hear. "But I'm glad Mrs Simpson was retiring. Otherwise we wouldn't have met."

He tightened his grip on her, not caring who saw them. He leaned into her and kissed her lightly.

"I knew you didn't leave my girl alone," Mrs Simpson said loudly. At least this time she had a smile on her face.

Everyone in the room laughed.

Someone put on some soft music, and Beau pulled her onto the make-shift dance floor. Their first-ever dance together.

He knew all eyes were on them, he could feel it. He was certain every cowboy in that room would be jealous of him, snagging such a beautiful woman.

She leaned into him as they moved around the tiny dance floor. He didn't know how to dance, so it was more like little shuffles. He had a sneaky suspicion she was the same but didn't care.

His hands rested on her hips, then slowly crept up her back. He felt an arm go around him, then she rested her head on his shoulder. He held onto other hand and squeezed it tight.

His heart rate hitched up, just holding her like this. He wished he could hold her forever.

He thought by now people would stop watching them, but he could feel their gaze burn a hole in his back. "Come on," he said, pulling her toward the house. "Get your jacket, and we'll find somewhere quiet."

* * *

Simone pulled her scarf up around her neck and zipped up her jacket. "Warm enough?"

She nodded but Beau pulled her closer anyway.

"The stars are so bright out here. They're like little Christmas lights flashing in the sky."

He grinned. "You don't have that in the city?"

"Never. And the moon – it's huge. We never see the moon like that."

Beau pulled her in to face him. He touched his gloved fingers to her cheek. "I hope you always get to see them that way," he said, then kissed her.

His kiss was gentle, despite the urgency he felt. "Simone, I…"

Suddenly, they were in bright light. Someone had turned on the floodlights and turned them their way. They obviously thought it was funny, but to Beau, it was far from it.

He pulled her close, trying to shelter her from the prying eyes. "What's going on?" She really had no idea.

"Invasion of privacy," he said, then grabbed her by the hand and pulled her along. They ended up in the vegetable garden his mother had planted many years ago. "This is as good as it gets," he said.

They stood amongst the turnips and potatoes. "Simone, I think I'm falling for you," he said. "And I get the impression you feel the same."

"I," She hesitated. And that worried him.

"Simone? If there's a problem, tell me now." His heart was racing, he didn't want to lose her. Was he pushing her too quickly?

She covered his lips with her fingers. "Shhhhhh, don't spoil it. Let's enjoy it while it lasts."

He stepped back out of her embrace. Was she for real? This was much more important to him than just a fling. He thought she'd felt the same way as he did. He was in this for the long haul. Forever.

"Is this a game to you," he asked. He couldn't disguise the annoyance in his voice.

She shuffled her feet before answering. "Is it to you?"

She'd totally avoided the question.

He grabbed her hand and pulled her along. "I'll take you back to the house," he said, still thoroughly annoyed, and even a little angry.

It felt as though someone had detonated his heart.

* * *

Why did she say that? She must have known it would upset Beau.

Simone closed her eyes, fighting the tears that threatened to break through.

Of course she knew it would, that's why she did it. Not to upset him, but to stop him in his tracks.

But why would you do that, when things were going so well?

The little voice in her head was relentless.

She knew the reason, although she didn't want to admit it – they were getting too close, and she was afraid.

She'd never had a relationship. Not a real one. She'd had dates here and there, but that was about it. She'd never gone past two dates.

Simone hadn't thought about it before, but now realized fear was definitely the reason.

Whether it was fear of becoming close to someone, or fear of being hurt, she wasn't sure.

But now she'd hurt Bea, and she wasn't sure either of them would recover intact.

There was no other way – as much as she loved it here, as much as she finally felt part of a family, she would have to leave.

Chapter Seven

Simone pulled her battered bag from the wardrobe.

She carefully folded the clothes Beau had bought for her and left them on the bed. Along with her beloved cowboy boots.

Her old worn clothes, she shoved into the bag, tears streaming down her face.

She felt hollow. As though a parent or sibling had died.

She clutched her chest. Why did she ever come here?

She knew how it would end. It always did – she always came out worse off than she went in.

She held back a sob.

The house was quiet – everyone had gone to bed. Beau had tapped on her door a few times, but she'd ignored him. Made out she was sound asleep. But how could she sleep after what she'd said.

And now she was walking out on him. Forever.

She thought about the times they'd been together. What it felt like in his arms. How her heart beat when he kissed her, and how she'd felt his presence before she even saw him.

Her heart ached.

Simone fumbled through her bag until she found her keys. She wasn't sure how far her beat up jalopy would get her, but she'd be away from the Silver Shoe Ranch, however far she got.

Away from Beau.

Her heart broke a little more, if that was even possible.

Her was the love of her life. *The one.* Her soulmate.

But she was too afraid to stay and make a life with him. Afraid of having her heart broken down the track. So, she decided to break her own heart right now instead.

* * *

Beau's heart was twisted in two.

He knew Simone loved him. Was one thousand percent positive of it.

So why did she say what she did?

This was never a fling to him. He would never do that to her. He was in it for the long haul, and he'd hoped she was too.

Despite what she'd said, he still believed they had a chance. Was certain she loved him the way he loved her.

He'd finally admitted it to himself, and it was probably too late.

He lay in bed staring at the ceiling. Sleep evaded him, and he just kept going over and over their conversation in his mind.

Nothing changed. The outcome was always the same.

She'd dumped him.

He'd tried to talk to her, but she'd ignored him. He wasn't going to barge in without an invitation, although he was sorely tempted.

He jumped out of bed and flung the curtains open, then stared at the scene before him.

The mountains were majestic against the cloudless sky, the moon peaking out behind them.

"I really love her, Mom," he said out loud.

He heard her voice as clearly as if she stood next to him. "Then go after her, Son. Don't let her get away over some silly little thing."

It was exactly what Marianne would tell him if she was here. He knew she would.

He pulled on his jeans and a pullover and went to her room.

The door stood open, but Simone wasn't there.

He found a note on top of the clothes he'd bought for her. "I'm sorry," it said, and was sighed "Simone", with a tiny heart over the 'i' the way she always did.

Pulling on some boots from his room, he rushed outside, but it was too late – her little jalopy, as she called it, was gone.

He wiped at his eyes.

It felt as though his heart was dying as it shattered into a million tiny pieces.

* * *

Simone sat back and slammed her hands to the steering wheel.

"Great time to die, you stupid car," she screamed. But no one heard.

She wiped at her tear streaked face, not sure if she was crying about Beau or the car, or both.

She hadn't even left the property yet. She was somewhere along the enormous driveway that led to the main road.

She'd been driving for a little over an hour when the car coughed and spluttered, and finally died.

There was no way for her to fix it – she knew nothing about cars – and there was no reception on her cell, so she couldn't call for help. Not that she knew who to call.

She looked about, not that she thought it would achieve much. There were no cowboys out and about at this hour. Although about now they'd be turning up for breakfast.

She swallowed back her guilt for letting them down.

It was too early for sunrise, and the sky looked eerie at this time of day. Another half hour or so and she would be reveling in its beauty.

She wondered if anyone had noticed her missing yet.

Okay, she wondered if Beau had noticed her missing. If *he* was missing *her*, because she sure was missing him.

She loved his scratchy beard in the morning before he shaved, and the way he came up behind her and hugged her tight before making his coffee.

The way he took a deep breath and declared "something smells good" while he waited for the jug to boil, set her skin to goosebumps.

When he hugged her when no one else was looking, it set her heart on fire.

Every. Single. Time.

So why did she leave?

Why run from the thing that's made her the happiest for a very long time?

Because she was afraid.

Not only of having her heart broken, but of hurting Beau.

The earlier she left, the easier it would be – for both of them.

She wasn't ranch wife material, not that he'd asked her, but sometime down the track it would come up. She just knew it would.

And how did she tell Beau about her nomad life? He'd led a stable home life, lived at the ranch forever, and had loving parents.

She thought about his mother, and her beautiful horse, Blaze.

She swallowed back a sob. She was going to miss Blaze more than she'd realized.

Simone put her fingers to her forehead. She was developing a migraine.

What if no one came looking for her, or no one ever found her, and she died out here?

It was rare for anyone to come out this way; they rarely left the ranch.

She lay down on the seat of her car to try and ease her migraine. Eventually she drifted off to sleep.

* * *

Beau was desperate.

He had no idea when she'd left, so didn't know where to start. His only hope was that her dilapidated car had finally breathed its last breath.

Hopefully not too far away, because he had no idea where she was heading.

He started up the helicopter as soon as it was light enough. He'd paced out the front as the cowboys headed in for breakfast.

"Help yourself today boys," he'd told them. "Simone's…" What should he tell them? He decided the truth was best. He took a deep breath. "Simone's gone," he said, his voice breaking.

"What did you do, Beau?" The accusation was clear.

Old Joe piped in. "Did you break that little girl's heart?" He could hear the anger in Joe's voice.

Others just shook their heads.

This was his fault, he knew it was true. He'd pushed her. Played his hand too quickly. She wasn't used to relationships, that much was clear, and he'd scared her off.

He'd filled the urn and put out cereal and bowls. The rest they'd have to do themselves.

Now that it was light enough, his mission began.

His brother Hank sat next to him. Beau had reluctantly accepted his offer of a lookout.

He'd created this mess and needed to fix it. He wasn't sure what sort of reception he would get from Simone when he found her. Or even if he would find her.

He swallowed hard at the thought.

* * *

They'd been searching for over an hour, and so far, no sign of Simone or her car.

Beau wasn't about to give up.

"What time did you say she left?" Hank asked.

Beau looked across at his brother. "I didn't. I have no idea. She could have gotten out onto the main road, but with that beat-up old heap, I doubt it."

Hank stared at him. "She could be in real trouble. Stuck in the middle of nowhere, perhaps."

Beau felt his blood begin to boil. "You are so helpful, Hank," he said angrily. "That's the last thing I needed to hear."

"Just tellin' it like it is, Bro."

"Keep your eyes down and find her." Beau didn't want to talk to his brother. He was beyond annoyed.

"What's that over there?" Hank asked, pointing to something somewhere in the distance.

Beau's heart beat ratched up, and he turned the helicopter in that direction. He was sorely disappointed. "It's just that old shed where we used to store the hay." He turned back to the direction they were heading before.

They sat in silence for the next hour, both of them concentrating on the ground below them.

Beau finally broke the silence. "We're going to have to return home soon. Fuel is getting low."

"Wait! What's that?" Hank pointed in the direction of what appeared as a small dot in the distance. "There, to your right," he said. "Looks like it's on the way out to the main road, so it could be your girl."

Beau looked in the direction Hank had indicated. His heart beat quickened. He hoped beyond hope it was her. It was difficult to tell this far away.

The closer they got, the more convinced he was it was her. But Simone was nowhere to be seen. And that worried him. A lot.

He hoped she hadn't begun to walk for help. That would be catastrophic.

"I'm going to land," Beau told his brother. "And check it out, but it sure looks like Simone's wreck."

He had to keep his head and make a smooth landing in the paddock. Luckily there was no stock around.

"I'm certain that's her car, but where is she?" He was getting really worried now.

They both sat waiting for the rotors to stop moving before leaving the cabin.

Beau was yelling her name before they were even close to the vehicle. She was nowhere to be seen. As he got close to the car and peered in the window, he breathed a huge sigh of relief.

There she was, sound asleep on the seat, seemingly without a care in the world.

He made a fist and banged on the window, startling her. He immediately regretted his actions.

She quickly sat up, rubbing her eyes, adjusting to the sudden light. She was talking, but he couldn't hear a word. He indicated for her to wind down the window.

Instead she opened the door. "The window winder doesn't work," she said sheepishly.

Impatiently, he pulled her out of the vehicle and dragged her into his arms. He hugged her tight. "What the hell, Simone?"

She pulled back, trying to get out of his grip. "I, I can't stay here," she told him.

He pulled her back into his arms. He was shaking with fear. Fear that he would never find her, but also the fear that she would reject him.

"I love you," he whispered in her ear. "I thought I was going to lose you today," he added quickly. "But I'm not going to force you into anything." He took a deep breath. "If you really want to leave, I'll help you, but I pray you won't leave."

She rested her head against his shoulder but didn't answer. He looked down to see her eyes were filled with tears.

Slowly her arms crept up his back. He lifted his hand to wipe away a tear as it trickled down her cheek.

"I love you more than words can express," he continued. "But I understand if you don't love me." His heart was breaking, and he hoped it wasn't so, but he wouldn't force her into anything she didn't want.

"I do love you," she said softly, then grabbed at his jumper, holding him tight. If the situation weren't so dire, his heart would be joyful. Right now, he was more concerned for her welfare.

"You could have died out here," he said quietly, knowing it was very true.

She nodded and began to cry. "I know that now," she said between sobs. "I don't know what I would have done if you didn't come looking for me."

He tightened his grip on her. "Of course I came looking. I couldn't marry you if you'd died out here."

They stood there for long moments, neither saying a word until he heard his brother clearing his throat. "We'd better get going, Beau. Everyone is worried."

Beau motioned him away. "So what do you say? Will you be my wife?" His heart beat rapidly waiting for her answer. The waiting was killing him.

Chapter Eight

Vern wasn't impressed at the news they were to marry.

"Now I have to find yet another cook," he said. "You're the best darned cook we've ever had," he told Simone. "But don't tell Mrs Simpson that." He said the latter conspiratorially, as if the older lady would hear.

"Why can't I continue cooking," she asked, confused.

"You can't do that when my grandsons come along," Vern said, as though it was all straight in his head. "Anyway, enough of that. We'll have to sort out living arrangements."

Beau held on tight to Simone. "I'm going to build a cabin for us to live in." His father looked confused. "For now we'll use one of the empty cow-hand cabins. We can stay there until our own house is built."

"You're not putting my daughter-in-law in one of those run-down wrecks!" Vern quickly came to her defense, much to Simone's surprise. "You should stay in the house until your own place is ready."

She'd never been inside any of the cottages the hired hands lived in, but knowing this family, she was certain they weren't wrecks. She had an idea of her own. "My room is perfect. Why can't we stay there for now?" Of course they weren't married yet, and she quickly back-tracked.

"I mean after we're married of course." She felt the color creep up her face. Beau squeezed her shoulder and grinned.

After Vern and Beau agreed to her suggestion, they began to work on wedding plans. Being the only cook on the property, she would have to do most of the catering, but Vern decided to ask Mrs Simpson to help out. Simone was not going to object.

"Now for a date," Beau said. "Let's have a Christmas wedding. I know it's only a few weeks off," he said. "But I think we can manage."

"I'd love to hang around here all day," Simone interjected, "But I have some baking to attend to."

She pulled out of Beau's arms and started for the kitchen. As soon as she was out of the room, she heard Vern talk sternly to Beau. "You've got a good woman there, Son. Don't lose her."

Simone smiled and hugged herself. She had no intentions of ever leaving Beau again.

* * *

With the wedding only days away, Simone and Beau were headed to Hidden Valley where her dress was being made.

Because time was precious, Beau piloted the ranch plane. It would save them over two hours in real time. The irony was not lost on Simone.

Only a handful of months ago she was sleeping in her car, wondering where her next meal was coming from. Today she was flying to the nearest town to have the last fitting for her extravagant wedding gown.

She'd protested of course. She was happy to wear an off-the-shelf dress, not necessarily a wedding dress. Beau was having none of it.

Vern had a few stern words to say too. He wasn't having his future daughter-in-law wear just anything to her wedding.

The result was a custom wedding gown, despite all her protests. If her parents had been alive, Simone would be ecstatic right now. Instead it was a bitter-sweet time for her.

He glanced across and frowned. "What's up? You don't look too happy."

She looked down into her lap. "Just thinking about my parents. I wish they'd been around to see us married. To meet you and your family." She swallowed back her emotion.

He nodded. "Yeah, I wish my mother was here too. But it is what it is." He reached across and squeezed her hand.

"I love you, Simone, and nothing is going to change that."

Her eyes welled with tears. "I love you too, Beau." A stray tear trickled down her cheek.

"What's this then," he asked, wiping her tear away. "Happy tears I hope. Not having second thoughts?"

She shook her head. "Never. You're the best thing that's ever happened to me."

After they landed, they headed toward the bridal shop. Beau tried to insinuate himself into the store. "Oh no you don't," Simone said sternly. "You can't see the dress until the wedding day!"

She dropped his hand and pushed him out the door. "Off you go. I'll call you when I'm ready." She stretched up on her toes, then brushed her lips across his more than willing mouth. "Go." And then he was gone.

* * *

Simone stared at herself in the full-length mirror. She didn't recognize this beauty.

Two staff stood around her. "It's stunning," she said, tears threatening to fall. "I don't know what to say."

The dressmakers grinned. They'd worked hard on this dress, Simone knew they had, and they'd fulfilled her every request.

The dress was made of off-white silk. She preferred that since pure white made her look ill with her pale skin. The bodice was Queen Anne style – a style she'd admired for as long as she remembered. She also didn't want anything too revealing, so it was the perfect design.

She'd asked for an A-Line dress, coming in taut across her waist and stomach, then flaring out, which suited her trim figure.

Pearls peppered the entire dress.

She stared at herself again; was the image staring back really her?

Despite her protests, Beau had paid for everything. She was beginning to understand the depth of wealth the Hadley family had, but it would never mean much to her. She loved the simple life.

After checking all the adjustments, and the length, the two women nodded. "Everything is perfect," Karina said.

"Now try the headpiece," Marie told her.

They lifted it above her head, and lowered it down, then pulled the veil forward. The headpiece completed the outfit. She was a real bride.

"Oh my Lord! Don't you cry!" Karina grabbed a box of tissues, then whisked the veil off her head.

Simone dabbed the tissue to her eyes. "I can't help it – it's all so beautiful." She blew her nose, then stepped out of her bridal gown.

"What about shoes," Marie suddenly asked.

Simone hadn't given them a thought. "I have cowboy boots," she said, lifting one foot for them to see.

Karina spun around, snatching up a box. "That will never do. Let me see again." She assessed Simone's foot then nodded. "These should fit."

The bride-to-be gaped at the Cinderella-style shoes now on her feet. She thought she might cry again. Everything was so surreal. It had all happened so quickly.

Marie frowned. "Let's put the dress back on to ensure the length is still okay with those shoes." They all breathed a sigh of relief when it was.

Karina whisked the entire bridal outfit away and boxed it up, ready for Simone to take home.

Home.

Silver Shoe Ranch was now her home. Her forever home.

Which was just the way she wanted it.

Epilogue

It was three days before Christmas, and also their wedding day.

Simone sat in the tiny chapel she'd visited so often over the last several months since she'd arrived. She prayed quietly as specially hired staff decorated the chapel in preparation for their wedding.

She prayed for the Lord's blessing over their marriage, and for healthy babies when the time came. She prayed for a sign that her parents, and also Beau's mother would be looking fondly over them on their wedding day.

"There you are!" Beau's worried voice broke through her prayers. "I thought you'd run off again." He looked so forlorn standing there.

She stood and pulled on her jacket, preparing to go out into the cold Montana winter.

"No such luck," she said, smiling, despite her nervousness. "I just needed a little alone time."

He watched the workers as they added small bouquets of flowers to the end of each pew. "It looks lovely." He pulled her close as they walked outside. "Nervous?"

"Very." She glanced at her watch. "It's nearly time to go and get ready."

Simone made her way back to her room. It was going to be tricky not letting Beau see her in the wedding dress before she made it to the chapel.

Vern met her at the front door. "I've got a surprise for you," he said quietly. "I hope you don't mind."

He held the door opened and she peered inside. It was her best friend Amy, who she hadn't seen for quite a while.

The two women squealed. Vern winced.

They ran into each other's arms. "I've missed you so much," Amy said.

Simone hugged her tighter. "I've missed you too."

"You needed a bridesmaid," Vern said, looking rather scared.

Simone turned to him and hugged him tight. "Thank you so much," she said between tears.

"Off you go. It's time to get ready," he told them.

They sat on the side of the bed. "I can't believe you're getting married," Amy said. "And living all the way out here."

Simone leaned over and hugged her again. "I can't believe you're really here. Those Hadley's really know how to surprise a girl."

"They flew me out here. No expenses spared," Amy told her. "Sent the money for the bridesmaid's dress as well." She stared at her friend. "I hope you like it," she said quietly. "It's your wedding but you had no choice on the dress."

"I'm sure I'll love it." Simone brushed her concerns aside. "Just having you here is amazing."

Amy checked her watch. "We'd better get a wriggle on. Time is running away."

She changed into her bridesmaid's dress, and pulled out her make up bag. Then quickly applied her own make-up.

Once finished, she applied Simone's make up – much more carefully. "Next up is your hair," she said. "All those years at beauty school are finally coming in handy."

She braided Simone's blonde hair and twirled it to fit perfectly under the bridal headpiece.

"And last of all," Amy told her, "The dress." She opened the lid to the bridal box that had been sitting on the bed.

"Oh my gosh, Simone!" She declared. "This is an amazing dress. If you're fiancée doesn't swoon seeing you in this, there's something wrong with him." She grinned at Simone and prepared to help her into the dress.

"Are you ready?"

Simone shook her head.

Amy reached out and took her hand. "You're shaking." She pulled her into a big bear hug. "Take three deep breaths."

She watched as Simone did just that. "Feeling any better."

"Maybe." She was still nervous but at least she didn't feel faint now.

Amy held out the dress, and Simone stepped into her fairytale wedding dress.

"I've got your something borrowed. The garter from my mother's wedding."

"Blue nickers for my something blue," Simone added. "Oh, and Beau bought me a necklace to wear today – that can be my something new."

"What about your something old?" Amy seemed quite concerned.

Simone scrounged through the bag she'd arrived with, frantically trying to find the tiny box she'd placed there so long ago. When she finally found it, she flipped the lid open. "My mother gave this brooch to me when I was ten. It was the last thing she ever gave me." Simone swallowed back a sob.

"Oh my, that is stunning." Amy took the box from her and pinned the tiny brooch onto the dress.

"It's not worth a lot, but it's very special to me."

"Of course it is." Amy closed her eyes. Simone could see the emotion she was fighting back. They were a good pair.

There was a tap on the door. "Ready?" Vern called.

"Is Beau gone?"

"Sure is."

She opened the door. Vern was a sight to behold – the old cowboy scrubbed up pretty good. Which got her to wondering about Beau.

"Have you seen Beau," she asked.

Vern grinned. "Don't you go worrying your pretty head about my boy. But I have to say," he took a deep breath. "You look a pretty picture, if I do say so."

She hooked her arm through his and they made their way to the little chapel, along with Amy. At first, she wobbled a little on the Cinderella shoes, but soon got the hang of it. Give me cowboy boots any day, she thought.

As they stood in the entrance to the chapel, Simone craned her head to see inside. The pews were filled, unlike this morning when she sat praying.

Everyone had been given the day off in honor of their wedding, and all the cowboys, and Mrs Simpson, sat inside, eagerly waiting for the bride to arrive.

As she looked to the front, she spotted her soon-to-be husband, in his Sunday best. His brothers Hank and Nash by his side.

She hoped someone had remembered the rings.

Suddenly the music began – her cue to proceed. Vern squeezed her hand. "You ready to do this?" he asked. He was her proxy father for the day. She was so grateful to him. If he hadn't stepped up, she would have been walking down the aisle alone.

Everything seemed to pass in a whirl, her head a buzz.

"Who gives this woman to this man?" Vern offered her to Beau. "I do," he said with a grin. With three sons, it would probably be the only opportunity he had to give a woman away, Simone realized.

As she stood next to Beau, he held her hand tightly, as though he would never let her go.

"Do you take Simone to be your lawfully wedded wife…"

"And do you Simone, take Beau…"

As if he knew she was feeling overwhelmed with it all, Beau put his arm around her waist. "I do," she said quietly.

"I now pronounce you man and wife. You may kiss your bride." Beau whipped her off her feet and kissed her passionately.

"Get a room, Son," Vern told him.

"I just may do that, Dad," he said, grinning.

Simone couldn't wait for the evening when they were able to consummate their love for each other.

* * *

As they walked down the aisle back out of the chapel, something came over Simone. She felt a presence. It was as though someone touched her on the shoulder.

She glanced around. No one was there – except for Beau, and he held her hand. They were arm in arm, and there was no way he'd touched her shoulder.

She stopped dead. She stared down at the brooch her mother had given her so long ago. "Mom, is that you," she whispered, so even Beau couldn't hear.

She shook her head. This was crazy. She was just overwhelmed was all. They continued making their way outside.

They stood in the entrance momentarily and let everyone pass them. It was tradition for the bride and groom to go out last.

Vern was the first to approach them. "Welcome to the family, honey," he said, and emotion threatened to overtake Simone. She reached forward and hugged her new father-in-law.

"Thank you," she whispered.

Vern stepped back, and everyone began to throw rice at them. Simone wriggled as it slid down her back.

Something touched her on the nose. She brushed it away.

She felt it again. She brushed it away again. She wondered if she had a spider on her face. Then she looked up, and around her.

It was snowing! It was her wedding day and it was snowing.

She wondered if this was the sign she'd prayed for. And then she knew – her parents were here watching over her and her new husband.

* * *

The wedding reception was held in the dining room.

Vern had decided to fly in a catering company after all. Mrs Simpson was practically part of the family, and he wanted her to enjoy the day.

She'd been there on the ranch since Beau was a little tacker and would want to see him married.

Amy sat alone on one of the tables, waiting for the reception to begin as the caterers worked in the background. She was tired after all the photographs they'd had to pose for. People were arriving in the dining room in dribs and drabs, and she was one of the few people there.

"Well hello there."

She turned to see one of the groomsmen standing above her. He was one of Beau's brothers if she was correct.

She extended her hand to him. "Hey. I'm Amy, Simone's friend."

"And I am Hank," he said. I'm one of Beau's brothers." He held onto her hand. "Would you care to dance?" He bowed theatrically, and Amy laughed.

"There's no music."

"I can fix that. Don't go anywhere." He sprinted to the back of the room and flicked a switch. Instant music.

He came back and stood in front of her again. "*Now* would you care to dance, Madam?" He took her hands and led her to the dance floor.

As his arms went up around her, Amy knew she was lost. She suddenly understood why Simone loved it out here.

The End

Thank you so much for reading my book – I hope you enjoyed it.

About the Author

Multi-published, best selling and award-winning author, Cheryl Wright, former secretary, debt collector, account manager, writing coach, and shopping tour hostess, loves reading.

She writes both contemporary and historical western romance, as well as contemporary romance and romantic suspense.

She lives in Melbourne, Australia, and is married with two adult children and has six grandchildren.

When she's not writing, she can be found in her craft room making greeting cards.

Links:

Website: *http://www.cheryl-wright.com/*

Blog: *http://romance-authors.com/*

Facebook Reader Group:
https://www.facebook.com/groups/cherylwrightauthor/